WAR
BY
OTHER MEANS

IDIARENO ATIMOMO

authorHOUSE®

AuthorHouse™
1663 Liberty Drive
Bloomington, IN 47403
www.authorhouse.com
Phone: 1-800-839-8640

This book is a work of fiction. All characters bear no resemblance to any character, living or dead

Published by AuthorHouse   05/31/2012

ISBN: 978-1-4685-8257-4 (sc)
ISBN: 978-1-4685-8258-1 (e)

This book is dedicated to the memory of my late father, Dr. Emiko Atimomo who taught me to love my country and always question the seemingly obvious.

PART ONE

AN UNBEATABLE OFFER

CHAPTER ONE

I T WAS THAT kind of morning Toju hated, misty and disheartening. The harmattan haze had suddenly descended on the city of Abuja. What made it particularly irritating for Toju was the unfamiliar occurrence of a traffic jam on Shehu Shagari Way which was just before the Three Arms Zone in Abuja. He had flown into Abuja the Saturday before. The weather was just beginning to get to him and he was grouchy as hell. Try as he could, he could never stop comparing Abuja with Warri his birthplace, the injustice of the architectural contrasts in both cities made his blood boil. Anyway, he thought, payback time was fast approaching.

As he drove, his mind drifted to that day he received a call from someone claiming to be the Chief of staff to the Delta State Governor. He had paused and jokingly told the fellow he wasn't in the mood for any crank phone calls. The voice on the other side insisted and said he was handing over the phone to the Governor just then.

An authoritative voice questioned through the phone "Is that Toritseju Omatsone?" the strength in that voice immediately put paid to the swinging movements on his swivel chair in his law chambers on Akin Adesola Street in Lagos; it wasn't everyday he heard his first name rendered in full. "Yes this is Toritseju Omatsone and you are?" "Mofe Amajuoritse, governor of Delta State" was the reply. Visibly shaken and wondering if he was having some kind of dream he greeted respectfully "Good morning. How may I help you sir?" After a brief pause, the governor replied,

"I want you to take care of a very delicate legal brief. It is rather unique and a very delicate one as it concerns the destiny of this nation and more especially your people in the Niger Delta." The way he said "your" made Toju shudder, though he was trying desperately to sound as though he received calls from State governors every other day. "Would you please elaborate on what you just said?"

The governor's voice rumbled through the phone, "I see that you are beginning to understand th e gravity of what I'm trying to say, to this end I have made arrangements for a face to face meeting. A car is on the way to pick you up from your office and take you to Murtala Mohammed Airport from where a private jet provided by one of our friends will bring you over here to Asaba, our state capital. If things work out as planned, you should be back in Lagos by 6pm, how about that?"

Toju was contemplating the way the governor used the word "we", he however responded quickly in the affirmative, his curiosity rising with every passing second.

"That settles it then", the governor said, "I want you to know we have a keen interest in your abilities and as such you have nothing to fear, alright?"

"All right Sir," Toju replied in a voice seriously lacking conviction. The governor dropped the phone after he restated his eagerness to meet with him.

Toju sat down for nearly ten minutes just reviewing that phone call and all that had been said, pondering what challenges lay ahead of him.

Little did he know how dramatically his life was about to change as he got into the black Mercedes G-wagon with the Delta state government license plates which had been sent to take him to the airport.

$$** \quad ** \quad ** \quad ** \quad ** \quad ** \quad ** \quad ** \quad **$$

Toju walked into the State House Asaba in confident and determined steps. He was a handsome man, of medium height with a body enjoying great muscle tone from frequent exercise. Already successful as a lawyer at the age of 36, he was good at what he did and he knew it. He was wondering just what kind of case he would be handling for the Governor as he was ushered into a boardroom by the governor's chief of staff.

Seated around the table were probably the most wealthy industrialists, corporate figures and politicians south of the River Niger. This was indeed "the" Power elite. Some of them he knew by name but most he could just faintly remember their faces from the National Elite magazines' center pages of social events his wife liked to collect.

At the foot of the table closest to him was Chief Tekena Tokubiye the textile magnate, beside the governor sat Chief Wale Adekanye, the billionaire who had made his billions when bitumen exploration kicked off in the Ondo-Ekiti axis. Senator Dafe Efetobo, an Urhobo High chief, was seated between two men he didn't know. He also recognized a two time federal minister who was now in political limbo, Engineer Chinedu Okafor.

A sudden movement broke Toju's survey of the room as he directed his gaze to the Delta State Governor who stood up and motioned Toju to a seat at the foot of the table. "Gentlemen", said the governor, "This is

Toritseju Omatsone, the man to whom we have decided to entrust a very important assignment." The governor looked at Toju and said,

"We have chosen you to hold brief for the people of the Southern states of Nigeria in court. We want you to contest the practice of Sharia legal system as a state religion in 12 of the northern states, what do you have to say?" Not a man of many words Toju thought but he said,

"May I ask sir, who is 'we'?"

To his utmost surprise everyone in the room burst into laughter and backslapping. He was totally surprised and felt so irritated by their laughter that he hit the table to get their attention once again. "What may I ask is so funny?" he asked.

Chief Efetobo spoke up, "Your keen mind is a delight to us my boy, I remember when I was a Young Turk lawyer myself back in the old days, when law was still law. A valid question you decided to pose and we are going to give you a valid response. I am sure that you are not unaware of the things that are going on in our country. Our brothers in the North have decided to ride roughshod on us till we are totally humiliated and dispossessed of all we hold dear.

The 1999 constitution has afforded them the loophole they needed to effect the introduction of Sharia Law as their legal system. This state of affairs is not good for business and is definitely not encouraging for nation building. The Federal government has adopted the head in the sand approach, believing that it is just an ill wind that will soon lose its' velocity and conveniently dissipate on its' own contradictions. We have not chosen this spineless path. This situation is bad enough for what it is and is even worse for what it portends. "We" are known as SOLUTION 1914. We believe the amalgamation of the northern and southern protectorates in 1914 by Lord Lugard on behalf of the British monarchy was a great mistake. The two parts of Nigeria have remained divided and seem to be hindering each others development with the northern political elite preying on the resources of the south. We are committed to emancipating our people from northern hegemony in whatever guise, civilian, military or legal."

Toju let some minutes go by as he tried to let all he just heard sink in. "So how do I come into the picture?" he finally asked. Chief Adekanye spoke this time,

"We believe that a document as immensely lacking in coherence as the 1999 constitution will definitely have some loopholes which *we* can also exploit for the benefit of our people, a sort of *war by other means* if you get our drift. The 1999 constitution was hurriedly put together by a desperate military government in retreat as we all know. We chose you based on your performance in Law School, specifically, the critique you wrote on the 1979 constitution and the Land Use Decree that has been adjudged to be one of the best thesis ever submitted to the Nigerian Law School. We want you to go to work on the 1999 constitution, tear it apart and put it back together, carefully going over it so as to discover whatever it is we can use as the final solution to end the economic and political assault of northern feudalists on our collective wealth South of the Niger."

For some two minutes there was pin drop silence in the room, only the humming sound of the split unit air conditioner could be heard.

"Before you say anything . . . ," Chief Tokubiye broke the silence, ". . . let me assure you that the necessary political and economic will and resources to carry out this assignment will be made available to you, all you have to do is ask." All eyes were focused on him, they were waiting for him to make a statement of commitment. At last he spoke, directing his response to the governor. "I don't believe I have so much to say. It appears you have done enough background checks on me to know that this is an offer I couldn't refuse, am I right?"

Turning his gaze away from Toju to the faces of the men around the table, the governor said, "Gentlemen. I believe we have found our man." He shifted his gaze to Toju and said "You are quite an intelligent man; tell me, do you play chess?"

** ** ** ** ** ** ** ** **

As he parked his car in the parking lot of the Supreme Court Library in the Three Arms Zone in Abuja, Toju was thinking how much his life had changed since that first encounter three months ago. A strange sense of destiny filled him in recent times. It was as if he had been born for this very purpose. He saw himself as being a sort of axe wielded by God against injustice. *This axe is going to cut deep.* Toju thought, as he put on the security locks of the car and walked into the library.

Chapter Two

TOJU WAS SEATED at his favorite spot in the Supreme Court library. A desk on the corner of the foreign publications aisle had become his daily work space. The place was fast becoming his home as he spent a greater part of regular working hours there. The librarians had begun to notice the middle aged man who was always so keen on being kept informed about every commentary on the 1999 constitution. He looked obviously well read and definitely financially comfortable. In fact, Chinwe, the secretary to the Chief Librarian had taken such a keen interest in him that she inadvertently talked about him to her boyfriend, David Ajiboye.

David Ajiboye had met Chinwe at the end-of-year party thrown by the Justices of the Supreme Court. He had introduced himself as a Chief Technician in the Federal Ministry of Works and Housing, Abuja. He was actually an undercover agent of the State Security Service (S.S.S). His brief was to establish a connection that would keep a monitoring eye on all happenings in the Supreme Court Complex. He had been supplied a dossier on Chinwe prior to "accidentally" spilling his drink on her handbag during the end of year party where they had met. He had quickly wormed his way into her heart, using skills of social engagement that even the S.S.S couldn't teach.

He had perfected these skills as a student activist in his undergraduate days. Winning elections on campus were complex; you seduced the secret fraternities, the religious groups, the campus magazines and then went in with a populist message for the rest of the school.

David and Chinwe had been having the usual "Abuja marriage" (the forced cohabitation of Federal civil servants as a result of housing shortages) for the past four months. Not once did Chinwe doubt David's claims about himself. A beautiful yet simple minded lady, Chinwe took people and situations at their face value. She had been talking endlessly about the latest Supreme Court scandal when she had let it slip about a certain man who it seemed was compiling a lot of research material on the 1999 constitution. David had wanted to overlook it when she first brought it up. He was used to hearing so much about who was dating which judge and who had jilted which Director of operations that he almost classified this new information in the same mental category he had created. He decided to probe a little further when he asked Chinwe what it was exactly that the man was interested in. She had promptly told him it was on all things related to interpretations of the constitution on derivation law, resource control, the onshore-offshore dichotomy and Sharia as a legal justice system. David's hunter instincts told him undeniably he was on to something here. He had promptly reported to his team leader who was covering his own beat on the National Assembly. The S.S.S had immediately mounted 24-hour surveillance on Toju Omatsone.

Toju on his own part was totally oblivious to those things that would have been telltale signs of being "shadowed" to a more sensitive person. He was doing what gave him the most pleasure, research on a scale he hadn't been involved in since his university and Law School days. As was his style, he had been forming his strong arguments but he always resisted the temptation to put them down in any logical manner until he had finished his work. This used to infuriate his friends in school and unknown to him he was also infuriating the S.S.S whose agents had been searching his suite in Transcorp Hilton Hotel Abuja without his being aware for the past three weeks. He had always loved playing around with the concepts in his head until he was definite about how he was going to present his facts in court. His presentations in court were generally regarded as being wonders to behold.

From his selection of his opening arguments, the order in which he called witnesses and even to his body language, everything about his court appearances were purposefully rehearsed.

Toju was just sitting down to take lunch at the cafeteria of the Supreme Court when his mobile phone rang. The call I.D display showed it was his wife on the line. "Jumoke hi," Toju said as he put the ear piece of a hands free kit in his right ear

"Toju how are you? You didn't call last night like you promised!" Jumoke had this way of getting straight to the point; it was one of the things that made her so irresistible. "I'm so sorry dear, I was so tired yesterday that when I got back to the hotel I just slumped on the bed and slept till 3 am when I woke up to hit the gym and plan for the day."

"I hope you're taking care of yourself. Tosan is starting to get to me with all his nagging about wanting his daddy." Jumoke paused and asked, "When did you say you would be flying to Lagos again?"

"Friday" Toju said, "I'm coming with the morning flight. Tell Tosan that daddy is coming home and he will only enjoy my visit if he has been a good boy."

"Here speak to him yourself, he's already contesting the phone with me," she said

"Hello daddy," Tosan was on the phone and he wanted the world to know.

"Strong man, how are you?" Toju asked. Totally ignoring the question, Tosan went to the heart of the matter, "Daddy will you buy me an airplane when you are coming back from Abuja?" "I'll buy you an airplane only if your mummy tells me you have been a good boy; now give the phone back to your mother." Tosan gave the phone back to Jumoke and scampered off to the sitting room that he had just converted into Lego land.

"Jumoke, I'm making some headway here and I'm sure I should be through by the end of the month" Toju said. "You said that last month and the month before" Jumoke fired back. "There is no need to talk like that Jumoke," Toju said before continuing, "You know I'm only spending this much time away from home because of the importance of this assignment. I miss the times we just talk about everything and nothing. Abuja is so boring. I wonder how I've managed this long without losing my sanity."

"I'll try to hold on for the next few days till you come, I'm sorry I sounded so mean but it's just that I'm missing you. I feel so alone sometimes even with Tosan around. I just sit on the bed and I'm laughing and crying at the same time as I remember all our fun times together."

"Hey, I'm not dead yet!" Toju screamed with a large smile on his face. Jumoke had a way of making him feel wanted.

"I'm coming home on Thursday at this rate! I love you dear, never forget I do, alright?"

"Alright I'll be waiting for you bye love" Jumoke said as she cut the call.

Toju went back to eating his food but became suddenly aware of some two young ladies sitting on the table to his left. They had apparently been listening to his conversation. He just smiled at them and continued with his lunch. He had been thinking of his Legal Chambers of late. It had seemed strange when he had explained his decision to his junior partners to take up the preparation of a brief for an unspecified client all by himself. They had all pressed to go with him but he had insisted.

He had kept in touch with them by phone but he was seriously missing the convivial atmosphere of his chambers. His "client", as he was wont to think of Solution 1914, had been sending a cheque of One million naira to his chambers every month since he got to Abuja. His client paid for all his hotel and phone bills. He had also been given a smartcard with what he could only think of as unlimited funds credited on it. It was obvious his client took this case as being top priority.

He was going to Lagos to give them an update on what he had found. They would get their money's worth. Toju thought, they definitely would.

**   **   **   **   **   **   **   **   **

On arriving Lagos, Toju was driven to the Delta State government lodge on Etim Inyang Crescent Victoria Island. Unknown to him, David Ajiboye was hot on his trail, a few cars behind the car that picked Toju at the airport. He had been given his marching orders when it became obvious that Toju was flying to Lagos. He had to quickly think up a line to sell to Chinwe to justify his traveling to Lagos. Shadowing Toju seemed to be getting very interesting. Imagine that! the man was actually driven to the lodge of that troublesome Delta State Governor, thought Ajiboye

Toju alighted from the G-Wagon that had picked him up at the airport. He was ushered into the waiting room of the governor's lodge. He had sat down for a few minutes when he noticed a strange movement to his right. It was almost an unnoticeable movement but he had noticed it. It must be some sort of closed circuit television, Toju concluded. Of late he had begun to wonder if he had not bitten off more than he could chew.

"Mr. Omatsone, please come with me," a voice said from behind Toju's head. He looked behind him to see a short man with hooded eyes and drooping shoulders. Quite a slight, Toju thought. He got to his feet and followed the man.

Two hallways and one staircase later, Toju was ushered into a boardroom. This time there were only three members of the original group he had met on that first day seated around the table. Chinedu Okafor and Mofe Amajuoritse were the only ones he could recognize, the name of the third man came to him briefly but it slipped out again before he could fix it to the face.

"What do you have for us Toju?" Okafor asked before Toju sat down. "I have made some findings which should help us win our case in court. By the time we institute the case in court our northern brothers would have got the message." For the next forty minutes, Toju outlined at length his brilliant strategy for securing the economic fortunes of the southern states without firing a shot.

** ** ** ** ** ** ** ** **

The three men were left in the boardroom. Toju had just gone out, to be driven home to his wife and son. Mofe Amajuoritse spoke to the man whose name Toju could not recall.

"When can you schedule a meeting with the Northern Elders?" The man was already studying his pocket organizer. "A weeks notice should be sufficient. A week from now, Monday the 13th to be precise."

"Perfect, the ball is now in their court, get our people informed about the meeting. Good day gentlemen." The governor stood up and walked out of the room.

CHAPTER THREE

A NEUTRAL GROUND HAD been demanded as the venue for the meeting. Lokoja, the confluence town in Kogi State with a deep significance in the history of Nigerian development into nationhood, had finally been chosen. It was the place where the amalgamation of 1914 had been effected. The country home of a retired military General from Lokoja town was the location of this meeting.

The cars started arriving at about 2pm that day. The inhabitants of the town were wondering which of the "big men" in the town was staging a wedding for one of his children to account for the number of exotic cars seen heading into the town. Judging from the license plates of these cars, it seemed every state of the federation had sent representatives to this meeting as was the case whenever there was a 'big man' wedding going on.

General Paul Wakili (rtd.) stood on the portico of his country home directing affairs and welcoming those arriving for the meeting scheduled to start at 4pm. It was the largest gathering of the Power Elite in Nigeria from the north and south. Security in the General's home was airtight. As the last of the guests arrived, Gen. Wakili walked towards the car park that had been temporarily converted into a base for the caterers who were to handle the dinner to be served after the meeting. He was giving them last minute instructions before he proceeded inside the house to be part of the meeting. So much was riding on this meeting, the General was thinking, I cannot afford to have anyone die of food poisoning in my home. "Hey listen to me," he was addressing himself to the proprietress of the catering outfit, "I hope you know what will happen to you and your staff if any of my guests should

so much as have a fever after eating dinner." He made a motion of sliding his hand horizontally under his chin from left to right indicating he would have them killed. "You understand?" he asked. "Yes sir" she replied. The General started walking back towards the house. The proprietress called all her staff together to pray, silently cursing her stupidity for taking this job.

** ** ** ** ** ** ** ** **

The meeting was already on the way; Mofe Amajuoritse was introducing the 15 members of Solution 1914 to the northern elders. This was a mere formality, as everyone in the room knew everyone else. They had all been in government or generally in the corridors of power for the past thirty five to forty years of the country's existence. Their children went to the same schools abroad and even married each other.

"We will go straight to the point and address the reasons for convening this meeting. At various forums, especially via the press, the members of our group and other men and women of Southern extraction have spoken out against the decision of 12 states of the North to implement Sharia as their legal system." Already murmurs were beginning to be heard from the Northerners in the meeting.

"Now wait for me to land before you begin to jump to conclusions. We did not call for this meeting to go on like a broken record on our views on that issue. Rather we come to intimate you with a resolution of our next line of action. We will not declare a "Christian State," this for us is just an exercise in amateur legislation.

We have found within the same constitution that produced the Sharia monster, our own Resource Control Monster."

** ** ** ** ** ** ** ** **

By the time the meeting ended and all the guests went to the dining room for dinner, the northerners were crestfallen. These Southern bastards have us by the balls, Ambassador Shehu Makarfi was thinking. They had eaten in silence quite in contrast to Solution 1914 members who were obviously in good spirits and even exultant in the face of their "coup", small talk was made around the tables; on the whole the atmosphere was contemplative.

As the last course was served, a note was placed in the hands of all northerners. On it was a phone number they were to call to ask about their next line of action. The only Southerner who noticed the distribution of the notes was Engineer Okafor; he noted it but said nothing.

After dinner, some of the guests retired to the rooms provided by Gen. Wakili in his palatial home. Most however got into their cars and headed to the hotels they had booked in town to rest before their homeward journey.

For Solution 1914, the night was a success. They had carefully outlined what they intended to do with their "chance" discovery in the 1999 constitution to the bewildered northern elite. The northerners argued at length and called their bluff but were painfully aware that they had been outfoxed this time. The southern elite assured them that running to implement their discovery was "Plan A" to them for now but could be shifted to "Plan B" or in fact no plan at all if the northerners were ready to entertain certain demands and concessions of some strategic ministerial appointments, oil prospecting licenses and a signed agreement specifying some yet to be privatized Public Corporations that were to be "no go" areas to northerners, the 5 oil refineries were top on that list.

The outrage of the northerners was clear. How dare they make such unholy demands and who told the Southern elite that they had as much influence on the federal government as they supposed? Governor Amajuoritse assured the northerners that they were capable of fulfilling their demands if they so wished. "It is our enlightened opinion that it would be better for us to settle this issue amicably by your accepting our demands than it would be for us to go ahead with our "Plan A" which is guaranteed to bring most of the northern states to their knees economically. As enlightened men I'm sure you can understand the implications of this. Make no pretence about "fighting for your people's rights". We all know that our greatest motivation in all our political posturing is primarily pecuniary. Think this over and get back to us soon."

And with these words the stage had been set for a trade off of the collective wealth of the Nigerian people. It was merely a commodity to be bargained for and shared by the nation's elite, north and south of the Niger. The general populace was unaware of the unfolding events but with such clandestine meetings was the future of Nigeria regularly determined by those the people called their leaders . . .

Toju Omatsone Solution 1914's innocuous accomplice, the Federal government of Nigeria, the State Security Service and the Nigerian power elite had taken the steps that would let loose the threatening avalanche that would eventually threaten the destiny of Nigeria.

PART TWO

GATHERING STORM

Chapter Four

It was another Wednesday morning. The Federal Executive Council meeting was soon to begin. Federal Ministers, Special Advisers, Special Assistants and Special Assistants to the special assistants had started arriving. Journalists were milling about, looking for some scoops for their papers. They were an irritating lot, at least to the ministers.

They always seemed to be hovering around them hoping to get one comment or the other. The ministers had given the press corps a very uncharitable nickname, which of course was top secret: The Vultures, always looking for some dead or dying poor soul to feed on. All they seemed to care about was getting a story on whose coattails they would ride to some form of national prominence.

The journalists too didn't care much for the ministers and other aides. They saw them as people who didn't really have much to offer the nation, they just happened to be in the winning party. But as it is with human nature, both sides always seemed to be in love with each other, the journalists needed their scoops and the ministers wanted photo opportunities on the front pages of the newspapers.

There were lots of hugging, handshaking, backslapping and gisting going on as the convivial atmosphere that had always preceded their Wednesday meetings was not missing today. At exactly 8:55am, the President walked in. A tall regal man, he was as patriotic as they come. He loved the nation and wanted improvements quickly. No one could fault his good intentions; his critics could only concede that he was too cautious when aggression was needed and too aggressive when diplomacy was needed. One newspaper columnist had called him the dog that no longer hears the hunter's whistle. The man was a paradox. Only such a man could have assembled such an equally diverse group of people to work for him.

"Good morning ladies and gentlemen," the President greeted. This was the signal for all journalists to be shepherded out of the room, as soon as they were out the President continued. "Who will lead us in prayer today?" he asked.

There was murmuring as the spiritual bankruptcy of the cabinet reared its head as they began to playfully goad each other on who was to pray.

"Okay, okay Mazi," the President said looking in the direction of the Finance Minister

"Pray for us and make sure you ask God to give us a balanced budget!" The room erupted in laughter.

Mazi Offodile took the prayer, which actually sounded more like a speech than a prayer.

"Once again good morning," the President continued after the prayer.

"We will go straight into the main business for today. Mr. Vice President what do you have for us on the privatization process?"

"Mr. President Sir, the fifth phase of the process is about to begin. Our consultants have finished their work and all that is needed is the final nod from the National Council on Privatization. I don't think there is need for much fanfare for this phase as the general public has become more enlightened on their need to get involved in the process. As you know sir, the problem now is the sudden withdrawal of bids for the core investor shares in some of the companies in the fourth phase. At least six of such bids have been withdrawn in the last week alone and it is already causing a buzz in the organized private sector, the credibility of the program is taking a bashing, as the whole thing looks pre-meditated. I personally mandated the National Security Adviser to carry out a preliminary investigation into it. He is supposed to meet with us, you and I, Mr. President, later in the day to give us a report. For now that is all there is to report on the privatization process." The Vice President then rearranged the files before him in a manner signaling a close to that matter.

"These are truly strange occurrences, I hope the NSA has something definite to report" the President said. He then called on the Defense Minister to give a report on his ministry. This culminated in a debate on the propriety of reducing fringe benefits to senior service men for a one-year period so as to offset the pensions of retired service men. On and on it went as each minister gave a report on his or her ministry. The President never seemed to miss a thing. At 11 am, he called for a short break so they could all relax for the next session. By the time the meeting was over, all the ministers and special assistants were in fact too tired to even give the press any sound bites. They had mandated the Solid Minerals Minister to brief the press on the outcome of the meeting.

**   **   **   **   **   **   **   **   **

The National Security Adviser, Alhaji Aminu Jiga, was in his office in the Aso Rock complex. The meeting he had attended in Arewa House

Kaduna last weekend was high on his mind. For the first time in any of the meetings of the Niima club, they were all perplexed. They were the last vestiges of what remained of Sir Ahmadu Bello's vision of an emergent and influential northern elite. Some called them the Kaduna Mafia. They had profited from every administration in Nigeria politically and economically. They in fact called the shots and were Kingmakers. For the first time they had been outfoxed.

The debates had been hot and impassioned. Most members declared they would never yield to such blackmail. "We should dare those kaffirs to do whatever they think they can!" screamed Alhaji Isa Galadima, "if they think we will back down, they must be crazy. If we capitulate today there is no saying what next they will be asking for. I say we tell them no!" some impassioned voices shouted their agreement. Aminu Jiga just sat watching everything. He raised his hand to speak and everyone kept silent for he was a highly respected member.

"From my humble assessment of our options, I think we should agree to their demands." Isa Galadima was up in a shot,

"How could you even say that Alhaji! Haba, Alhaji have you been compromised?" Jiga gave him a cold stare and this unnerved the boisterous Galadima, he promptly took his seat.

"For many years we had our way in this country" Jiga said. "This has largely been due to our unbroken solidarity, singularity of purpose and our ability to correctly gauge the move to make that would best protect our interests. We have also been aided by the broken ranks of our Southern brothers. They have somehow realized this and come together, but their unity is under a different banner than that which really motivates us. We see ourselves as being honorable men of a distinguished race. We fancy ourselves as being born to rule." To this, many of the people seated nodded their heads in approval.

"They have no such conceptions. Their motivation is primarily pecuniary. They would sell their mothers at the right price. For now this makes them formidable. One of the first things we will have to do is to find a way to break their ranks. Till then, I suggest we give in to their demands. This may look like capitulating but in truth we are only buying time. To yield is sometimes the first step in attacking an enemy. We give them a few pawns to lay them up to capture the queen. We stall for time to plan and strike back. Our strike back may take the form of theirs, simple and pleasant, a proposal to be made or we might go ahead with a violent take over once again of governance." All present were taken aback by Jiga's words. Another coup d'etat? 'Surely not at this time' was the dominant murmur that ran through the seated assembly. Jiga continued.

"I must confess that is an unpleasant option for me as well, I'm not too keen on it but I keep it as a possibility. The point is that we must respond to this challenge with all at our disposal, when the time is ripe. As a first step I am going to be resigning as the NSA next Wednesday."

Ahmed Muazu spoke up, "Alhaji, truly your plan seems to make sense but it is too vague a plan. If we disengage from politics and business like they want us to for even a year I doubt if we could ever regain what we've lost.

The surest way of recovery would be by coup d'etat and I for one will never support one." Muazu and Jiga eyed each other. They had never been friends. He can never miss an opportunity to spar with me, Jiga thought. He finally said "Be rest assured Alhaji Muazu, I don't want a coup either. Now if we refuse their demands what do you propose we do? Let us hear a solid plan of action if you have one." All eyes rested on Muazu, he was a shrewd businessman but not a quick thinking man like Jiga. He simply stared into space thinking of what to say. Jiga made this pause seem like an acknowledgement of his superior thinking and said

"If there are no more dissension's I would like to propose we set up two committees on this matter. One will be an implementation committee charged with the task of ensuring at least a reasonable looking acquiescence to the demands made on us. It should appear to them that we accede to their demands by the moves this committee will orchestrate. The second committee will be our Response Committee; they will investigate our next move looking at all the options available to us and their likely contingencies. Their specific mandate is to give us a bigger weapon than the ones we presently hold, a kind of final solution. We must hold all the aces when the dust settles or else we will be in no better position than we are now."

A leader had emerged and it seemed all acknowledged the fact. Perhaps all was not lost after all. There were nods of approval and side comments of support. Jiga spoke up once again "I would like to nominate Alhaji Muazu to head the implementation committee." There were spontaneous outbursts of laughter and shouts of agreement as the nitty gritty of the details were beginning to emerge from the minds of these seasoned kingmakers.

** ** ** ** ** ** ** ** **

Jiga again read through his letter of resignation. It would come as a shock to the President, but what did he care? His task was over here. He would simply send it to the President's office and head straight to Zaria his hometown. The report he had been asked to submit on the withdrawal of core investors in the privatization process lay before him. He had been tempted to put the real reasons for those events in the file but had been advised by the implementation committee not to. Instead he was going to present a massive hoax tale. Let them pick up the pieces, by the time we make our move they might not even be in power any more. Power was his ultimate goal, he loved and worshipped it. Scheming for power was merely a game he played. Surely I will emerge from this situation better placed in the new power equation he thought as he closed his suitcase, picked it up and headed towards the door.

CHAPTER FIVE

TOJU HAD BEEN in Lagos for about three weeks and he still hadn't heard from Solution 1914 since his presentation to them. He had tried calling the contact number he had been given at his first meeting with them but all to no avail. His calls kept going to an answering machine; he had even tried calling the governor through his Chief of Staff but was always told that the governor would get back to him soon.

To cap it all, Jumoke had started telling him she was sure someone had been in their house at least twice when they were not in. He had tried to dismiss it in his usual manner; he had chided her and said she had been watching too many films. Now he wasn't so sure, the whole thing had begun to give him the creeps.

He picked up the last edition of Applause magazine his wife had bought and leafed through the glossy picture pages. It suddenly dawned on him while staring at the picture of one wedding that most of the guests were people that you would never expect to see together and discussing in such an intimate way. It was the wedding of the daughter of a former Head of State, a real 'who is who' wedding. He could see the wives of sworn enemies on the political battlefront engaged in deep discussion. These people are never really against each other, Toju thought, they only appear to be at loggerheads but in fact they are all friends.

His mind also began to ponder on the goings on in the country in the past few weeks. It seemed there was an orchestrated pullout of northern businessmen and politicians from some hitherto exclusive areas they had previously dominated. The dailies were awash with conspiracy theories of all sorts. The Federal government had been thrown into a quandary trying to explain these events but to no avail, tensions were rising all over the country. Toju's keen mind had somehow linked these series of events to his presentation to Solution 1914. Barely two weeks after that, those strange occurrences had begun and then to cap it all, he had not been contacted since then. Things were not looking good.

He decided to send a brief explanation of the events leading up to the present time to an old friend Charles Ofili, who was now an editor with the Empire newspapers. He had sealed the envelope and even stamped it. He was now only wavering between sending it or not. He decided to send it but not right away, he thought. There was no point acting impulsively when he still wasn't sure what was going on yet. He would give it to his secretary and tell her to mail it only when he called and told her to. Yes, that's what I'll do, Toju thought as he reached for the glass of juice on the table before him.

** ** ** ** ** ** ** ** **

David Ajiboye was wondering what the report he had submitted on his surveillance of Toju Omatsone was going to do to his chances of a promotion. He had come to the conclusion that Toju was involved in some sort of subversive plot against the state. This plot involved the Delta

State Governor and some other influential Nigerians; the actual specifics of the plot were still a mystery to him. He had asked for a larger-surveillance team that world work interdependently across the nation to sniff out what the plot was all about. Still no word from HQ, David thought. Don't these people know that time is of the essence? For now he was still on Toju's trail. He would not let this fish out of his sight.

** ** ** ** ** ** ** ** **

"Gentlemen it has come to my attention that Mr. Omatsone has been making calls to my office, trying to fix an appointment to see me. Doubtless he is waiting for the go ahead to institute the case he prepared for us in court". Mofe Amajuoritse was addressing a full meeting of Solution 1914.

"It seems he has taken this thing as a form of personal crusade for righteousness. This was something we didn't consider before taking him on. I believe this could be a slight problem for us. We have started achieving our aims and I believe we are content to leave things the way they are. The economy is up for grabs now and we haven't fired a single shot or instituted the case yet". He paused, took a breath in and continued. "I believe we should call this man in and pay him off for his services before he goes on a self righteous mission to save the world". There were some guffaws around the table in reaction to this but the governor continued,

"However, I have a gut feeling this young man will not be easily silenced, money is no more a motivator for him. There is nothing as dangerous as a man who believes he is defending a righteous cause. I therefore suggest that a permanent solution should be considered if the first option fails. We can't afford to take any chances".

The room was dead silent. Many of these men were businessmen who were not used to such subterranean intrigues. Kill the man? Hell no, most of them thought. Chief Adekanye spoke for many of them

"Mofe don't you think that is a bit extreme? Surely there have got to be other ways of ensuring his compliance?" He leaned forward expecting an affirmation. He was to be disappointed.

"How do you think your businesses would survive the instability that would result from that case being instituted in court? How do you think the northerners would react to their agreement with us being flagrantly abused? How would you like your names all of over the front pages of newspapers all over the country as men who are plotting to destabilize the state? How would a treason charge sit on your neck sir?" Governor Amajuoritse had stood up with the rising tempo of his words. He was taller than most of the men in the room, in the standing position while they sat, he looked like a headmaster instructing his pupils.

"Gentlemen, I'm not too keen on doing that but I will not hesitate to ensure that our interests are protected. If he stands in our way, he will be removed".

It is sometimes said that silence can also stand for agreement. On this day silence reigned. Dr. Jekyll had become Mr. Hyde before their very eyes. The seeds of disunity had been sown in the group from now on; their purposes were no longer in sync.

The discussion moved to some other areas but there was now uneasiness in the room. It would linger in their hearts even after they dispersed.

** ** ** ** ** ** ** ** **

The response committee had submitted a report to the house. It was written like a document of war. It had three basic aspects: policy, strategy and tactics of response. In the policy section they had pinpointed who the enemy was, why they had to respond and when they should respond. The strategy section outlined the "war on the map", the operations needed to effect the policy by moving available forces to enable the total imposition of their will on the enemy. The tactics section outlined the actual methods of engagement and those to spearhead them.

The discussions had been stormy yet fruitful, the document was approved and another implementation committee was set up to bring the plan to reality. Jiga was pleased; he had unanimously been chosen to direct this project. He had already started organizing the media blitz of orchestrated scandals that would blow open the flank of Solution 1914, from messy sex scandals to numbered accounts in Switzerland exposing a trail of looted resources. They want to play dirty, well two can play, Jiga thought. That would just be the beginning of their troubles.

** ** ** ** ** ** ** ** **

"What in the Lord's name is happening in this country?" The President was asking no one in particular. Seated around him were the Vice President, the new National Security Adviser (NSA), the Inspector general of police, the Director General of the State Security Service (SSS), two Federal ministers (Internal affairs and defense) and his special assistant on state security.

"The privatization process is in shambles, my ministers, advisers and ambassadors are resigning. Nigerians are in an uproar, conspiracy theories flying left and right, for God's sake what is going on?"

The SSS director requested permission to speak,

"Sir our operatives are presently working round the clock trying to find out the root cause of these issues. We have some leads we are trying to follow up on, till we have something definite however conjecture reigns.

"What are the leads you have man, speak up" the Presidents legendary temper was coming to the surface.

"We have an operative who has reported a strange link between the timing of the bid withdrawals with a meeting of very strange bedfellows in Lokoja about a month ago. Some political and business heavy weights from all over Nigeria were at that meeting hosted by Gen. Wakili (rtd). Not only that, another of our agents sent in a report indicating some sort of plot involving resource control agitation being hatched by the Delta State Governor and some other prominent Nigerians. He is still following it up and we are assigning more agents to spread the net of that particular investigation.

"Get me the Delta State Governor on the phone now" the President said to his special assistant.

"Mr. President" the Vice President said, "I don't think that would be particularly wise right now, it might preempt the ongoing investigation. What would you ask him? If he was responsible for what's going on? Surely even if he knew anything about it he would promptly deny and begin covering his tracks. I suggest we sit tight, get the necessary information that would allow us make informed decisions and then we promptly move in to contain the situation I believe this should be handled with as much tact as possible" The President was calmer now, dissatisfied but calm.

"I guess that would be the best thing to do. Gentlemen, what do you think?" they all expressed their agreement. The new NSA however had something to say, "Sir, in the light of what we now know, the problem seems to be on a national scale. I would suggest that daily reports coming to the SSS and other security agencies from their field agents be sent to the office of the NSA. As I have a more direct and frequent access to the President. Our responses will need to be coordinated from such a central point. This is my suggestion."

"Yes, yes I agree", the president said. If there was anyone he trusted it was his new NSA. When things go wrong it's always good to have your friends around you, he thought.

"Daily reports should be sent to the NSA. If there be need for us to come together again you will all be alerted. Good day gentlemen".

He motioned for the new NSA, Engineer Chinedu Okafor to wait behind as everyone else left the room.

CHAPTER SIX

OJU SLOWED HIS car down to obey the traffic warden on the road. At last the much awaited phone call from Governor Amajuoritse had come through that morning while he was at work. He was on his way to the Governors lodge. He had rejected the offer of a car coming to pick him up and insisted he would drive himself there.

The blaring horn of the car behind him brought him out of his reverie, he switched the car back on and moved the car back on the road, the warden had waved him on but he hadn't been looking. He finally got to the lodge on Etim Iyang Crescent Victoria Island. On getting to the gate, he informed the guards that the Governor was expecting him. One of them came close to his car and said

"Good day sir, we know you are being expected but we cannot let you drive into the compound so just find a place to park and come in". This is what you get when you insist on driving yourself here Toju thought as he put the car in reverse and found a free parking space for the car.

The foot gate was opened and he was led in. This time around he was taken directly to the Governors office. He was standing by the window when Toju came in. "Welcome Toju" he said as he walked over to Toju, extending his hand for a handshake. They shook hands and sat down facing each other, the governor sat on the other visitors' seat instead of his chair behind the desk.

"First and foremost, I must apologize for not getting across to you for awhile. It hasn't been easy leaving the state. I hope my apology is accepted" the governor said. "Accepted", Toju said at the same time was wondering when the man had become so considerate.

"I've been waiting for your go-ahead to institute our case in the Federal High court Abuja. It is my view that we should proceed with the case as soon as possible" Toju said

"Well you see Toju, err . . . events seem to have overtaken that particular matter", the governor said and continued

"I'm sure you can note the level of instability in the country now, we don't need to do anything to make it worse than it presently is. Besides, we have come to the conclusion that the case should no longer be continued, we don't want to heat up the system" Toju sat down dazed for a few minutes before he spoke

"If I recall sir the whole idea "was" to heat up the system, to offer a counteracting response to the Federal government's foot dragging on the issues affecting the people of the Niger Delta. So what is to become of the yearnings of the people? Are their pressing needs now expendable? Are you abandoning the people so that you don't rock the boat? I hope I'm getting you well, sir. Are you saying the case should no longer be prosecuted at all or are we to postpone it for a more opportune moment?"

"Actually Toju, we no longer have any intention of going along with the case you have meticulously prepared for us now or at any other time" The governor spoke with finality

"However we are committed to rewarding you for the effort you have put in so far. We have this attractive severance package for you". The governor handed over an envelope to Toju who calmly opened it and removed a cheque from inside it. Fifty million naira, my God, Toju thought.

"That is just a token of our appreciation; we are also looking into doing some other things for you as time goes on"

So many thoughts were coursing through Toju's mind. His mouth was being stopped. He felt used and dumped. This must be how prostitutes feel after collecting the reward for their "labor". He looked at the cheque one more time. I didn't take this case for the money; I took it up because I believed this was my God-given chance to liberate my people from the shackles of slavery in their own land he thought. He was sorely tempted but what he must do was now very clear.

He stood up and stared down at the governor, stretching the envelope back to him he said,

"I'm tempted to take the cheque and walk away but I cannot. This is how slaves are made. For how long must we continue to sell our people out? I believe strongly that the people of the Niger Delta stand to gain much more from the prosecution of this case than whatever these few millions can do for me. Don't bother increasing the price, I'm not for sale" He was already at the door when the governor said

"Hold it there soldier, you have chosen a particular road, I hope you are prepared for what you meet at its end. You are not dealing with small fry here. You are dealing with some of the most powerful people in the country. If I were you I'd reconsider, take the cheque and walk away before things get out of hand"

"Is that a threat?" Toju asked.

"Call it what you will but I'm sure you know what I mean" the governor replied. They stared at each other for some minutes. Finally the governor said, "Watch your back Toju Omatsone, watch your back"

"I definitely will", Toju said as he closed the door and walked out of the lodge.

** ** ** ** ** ** ** ** **

David Ajiboye was thinking it strange that Toju had driven to the lodge by himself this time. This wasn't a fluke occurrence, it must mean something. He was still musing on this when Toju come out of the lodge and walked toward his car, a green Toyota RAV4 Jeep. By now David had been joined by two other SSS agents, it was one of them that alerted him to Toju's countenance, "He seems mighty worried about something sir" "Hmmn, we'll see about that," David said as he turned the ignition of the car. He had barely reversed the car when two men came out of the lodge, got into a car and started following Toju's car.

"Looks like we have company", David noted as he allowed a reasonable distance between the two cars. It was obvious the people in the car didn't want Toju to know they were following him. What does this mean? David was trying is think critically. It seems there must have been some sort of fallout in their camp. The guy comes here on his own; he leaves looking disturbed; now he is being trailed by the governors goons who are obviously trying to be unseen. Something isn't right with these guys anymore.

** ** ** ** ** ** ** ** **

All his suspicions were true after all, Toju thought. These guys were not straight with me from the beginning. They obviously had their own agenda. He was on the roundabout just before the Chevron headquarters in Lekki: He had called his chambers and told them he was going home for the day. He was already close to Victoria Garden City (VGC) where he lived when he became quite definite that he was being followed. He usually would never have noticed but he had become quite security conscious of late.

The blue Honda Accord had been following him since he left the Island some minutes ago. He was trying to think of what to do to shake them off. The first thing he knew was that he wasn't going home anymore; he drove past VGC and increased his speed. The Honda paced up behind him. They are definitely on my trail thought Toju. As he approached one of those demarcations that allowed you to move from one side of the dual carriage road to the other, he suddenly pulled over and parked his car. The Honda didn't have a chance; it just shot past him with the aim of slowing down ahead. Toju waited until the car had stopped and the engine was off before he suddenly fired his engine, deftly got back on the road and crossed to the other side of the carriage way. He started speeding back towards the island.

From his rear view mirror he could see the men in the Honda were too dazed to effectively respond, before they could cross the road he was gone. I'm on the run now Toju thought *how did I get myself into this mess?*

PART THREE

SACRIFICIAL LAMBS

CHAPTER SEVEN

Toju had dropped his car in one of the parking lots in the 1004 flats in Victoria Island. He went out through the second gate and walked down the road and turned left. He walked into a branch of Paradise Bank, went straight to the Automated Teller Machine and withdrew ₦60,000 cash from his account all in five hundred naira notes. He didn't want to go through the tellers; there was no saying how wide the net had been sprung already.

He walked out of the bank and went into one of the fast food outlets on the same street. He was hungry but above all he needed some time to think. He bought a pack of chicken and chips and went to the back of the sitting area so he could see the door from where he was sitting. This spook business is getting to me thought Toju, I'll have to call Jumoke and tell her what just happened. He had barely started eating when the headline of a newspaper on his table caught his attention.

CHINEDU OKAFOR, NEW NATIONAL SECURITY ADVISER, OTHERS SWORN IN. That name sounds familiar, thought Toju as he reached out to pick the paper. A picture of the people being sworn in was on the front page. He immediately recognized Okafor. My God what has the President done, thought Toju, bringing in one of these hawks as his NSA? The man must be nuts or maybe . . . . The President is in on the whole thing too. Right now he just couldn't think straight. One thing he was sure of was that the Presidency was one place he wouldn't be safe.

He finished his food and walked out of the eatery. I've got to find some safe place to stay, and then I'll call Jumoke. Suddenly a text message came into his phone. It was short and to the point:

"We have your wife and child. Call this number now and give us your exact location" Toju's skin broke out in goose bumps; he was scared but also annoyed. How dare they bring his family into this? He walked back into the fast food joint, took a seat and called the number. It rang twice before it was picked up. Toju said,

"Let me talk to my wife". A gruff voice said, "You're in no position to make demands, just tell us where you are".

"How am I even sure they are there with you? Until I talk to them, no show" said Toju. Just then his phone beeped to show him there was another call coming in. Toju put the first call on hold as he took the second call.

"Toju are you home yet? I dropped a message with the guards to tell you I was going out briefly" Jumoke said.

"No I'm not at home, where are you Jumoke?"

"I'm on my way home, Tosan is with me. Toju what's the problem, you sound worried?" "Now listen very carefully Jumoke don't go home, go any where else but home, not now. My clients have sent their assassins after me but I shook them off. They just called me now to threaten me saying they had you and Tosan with them"

46

"Oh Toju what kind of trouble is this, where are you now? You know I told you someone had been in our house! Where am I going to go now?" "Just go to your sister's house for now" said Toju,

"I'll call you back soon okay?" He didn't give her a chance to reply as he ended the call and took the first call again "Now listen to me you devils! Go tell your bosses that they can't move me one inch from what I'm going to do. I'm going to blow up the whole thing in their faces. Yes and while you're at it, say hello to my wife!" Toju laughed long and hard before he cut the call.

** ** ** ** ** ** ** ** **

It was already three days now since Toju dropped out of circulation. David had to admit, the guy was good. The way he had dumped the guys trailing him had been impressive. Unfortunately he had also been unable to catch up with Toju too. David had assigned men to watch Tojus' house, his office and someone was already working on piecing together the information needed to find out where exactly he might be hiding.

Still no clues, his car had however been found in the 1004 flats complex. This guy was proving to be a very resourceful chap, bringing him in for questioning was the only option in sight for making any progress with this case. Obviously, Toju had fallen out with the Delta State Governor, it's also obvious they intend to kill him or do him harm. His life was in danger; we must ensure he stays alive at all costs, thought David.

He had called Chinwe yesterday, she was mad at him but she still loved him. Funny enough he was beginning to think he loved her too. Maybe love is still too heavy, David thought, all I can safely say is that I miss her and coming from me, that is something. He hoped to tie up this case soon so he could return quickly to Abuja.

** ** ** ** ** ** ** ** **

Alhaji Jiga invited Lt Gen. Datti. Muktar, the Chief of Defense Staff, for lunch in his suite in Transcorp Hilton hotel Abuja. As they ate, they engaged in small talk. After the meal, Jiga got up and called General Muktar to join him in the lavishly furnished sitting room.

"I'm sure you're curious as to the real reasons why I called this meeting" Jiga said as soon as they were seated.

"Without a doubt, I can even say I'm more than curious". They both laughed at that.

"I'm sure you are not unaware of the present state of things in the country.

General insecurity and instability, the economy is experiencing one of the most turbulent times we've ever had, inflation is rising faster than what the government seems to be able to cope with, in fact the government is appearing to be more inept by the day. They've lost a grip on governance. The truth is that many of us are not pleased with the trend of events in the country. The people are losing faith in the political class; Scandals are breaking out daily highlighting the bohemian lifestyle of the political class, most especially our southern brothers". At this Jiga paused so he could read Muktar's reaction. Muktar simply maintained his unfazed look, waiting for Jiga to continue. This one's a tough customer thought Jiga as he continued,

"The Northern Elders have come to the conclusion that a change is needed". There was a brief pause as both men sized each other up.

Am I really hearing right? Muktar was shocked though he kept a straight face. These people haven't learnt anything. Do they really think the military will get involved in their mess anymore? There is no way I'm

48

going along with this, these people must be taught a lesson that the times have changed. He must play along, at least long enough to know who and who exactly is involved and with evidence too. He finally spoke,

"We have actually been waiting to see what our elders had to say about all this mess. The military is not happy with this drift either. Are you suggesting a coup?" Jiga was too pleased to think straight,

"Yes, yes that's what we are thinking of but of course we need you to coordinate the movements, we would prefer a palace coup, you take over power and you promise to hold elections in a year's time. Of course a northerner will win these elections we have been ordained by Allah to rule, the country has always had peace when we were ruling. It is for the good of the whole country. As the most senior officer you will become Head of state. When you hand over power you would have become an international statesman for having restored the democratic process", his eyes were aflame with ambition as he spoke. Muktar was so disgusted he almost felt like slapping him but he resisted the impulse.

"I will need to meet the commanding officers of the major military divisions before we know how we will bring the plan to fruition. I will get back to you but I'd like to meet some of the other Elders along with you the next time we meet, will that be possible?"

"For sure, that can be arranged" Jiga said as he began wracking his brain to find how he was going to convince some of them to come. Yes, he knew what to do. He would simply say Muktar approached him with the idea of the coup.

"If that is all, I should be on my way now." Muktar said as he got to his feet,

"I'll call to let you know when I'm ready for the meeting. May Allah help us all" They shook hands and Jiga saw him off to the door.

CHAPTER EIGHT

OJU HAD CHECKED into Cool Me Down Motel, a real rundown establishment in Mushin, on the mainland of Lagos. I've seen them all he thought, from 5 star hotels in Abuja to a $^1/2$ star motel in Lagos! My memoirs should make for quite exciting reading he thought grimly. Jumoke had moved in with her sister in Ikorodu, no one would think of looking for her there, at least I know she's safe thought Toju.

He had spent time thinking of what should be his next line of action. Reporting to the police seemed unwise for now, there's no saying what kind of rap they've put on me to ensure I'm picked up. He had also thought of getting down to Abuja and instituting the case immediately but on second thoughts he'd seen that to do so would be to unnecessarily expose himself, they might be waiting for him there too. It seemed the only option open to him was to find a way of blowing the whole thing open to the public. But should he reveal everything or just some parts of this weird tale? The way things stood now he'd have to reveal everything, every move, every meeting, everyone involved, who said what, when and where.

The report he'd prepared for Charles Ofili was still with him, he had taken it back from his secretary when he'd received the summons to see the governor. He had thought there was no longer a need to post it and had put it in his briefcase when he went to see the governor. Now all he had to do was flesh it up and be more specific. He wouldn't post it, he'd go and see Charles himself.

He took the empty sheets he had just bought and began writing all he knew about Solution 1914, its members, aims, and activities.

** ** ** ** ** ** ** ** **

"If all our officers were like you, the future of democracy would forever be assured" the President was speaking to General Muktar, also present in the room was the Vice President. "To think that Alhaji Jiga could actually be involved in a coup plot at this time in the life of the nation is very unfortunate. I guess this explains his resignation and probably the resignation of some of the other northerners in my government." The different challenges his administration had faced had taken a toll on the President. Slouching shoulders and a less cock sure choice of words had replaced his once hefty frame and combatant postures. He sighed deeply and looking to the Vice President asked

"So what do you suggest we do?" As a retired officer, the Vice President spoke from his background, "It's obvious we are faced with a clear case of treasonable felony. All we have to do now is to find out all those involved and get evidence to establish the fact of treason. These people are powerful but no one ought to be more powerful than the state".

"Sir I agree with the V.P, I think its time our people learn that no one is above the rule of law", Muktar chipped in. "Wouldn't that unnecessarily stir things up among northerners? Do you think they'd believe Jiga was really planning a coup?" the President asked

"I guess that's where General Muktar comes in" said the V.P.

"You will have to find a way of obtaining concrete evidence of Jiga's involvement and that of all his co-travelers. I believe the time has come for us to smash all these rival authorities to the supremacy of the state. Mr President, this particular occurrence demands firmness; we can't afford to sweep it under the carpet. Yes, there might be a few protests but at the end the truth must bear us witness".

"That's true, very true. Now we must inform the NSA and hear what he suggests. The sooner we move to contain all those involved the better. Needless to say, for now mums the word" The very tired President said.

** ** ** ** ** ** ** ** **

Engineer Chinedu Okafor had been going over the security reports the SSS had been sending to his office. Apparently they had already found a link between Toju and Solution 1914. The SSS agents assigned to him had lost him just about the same time Mofe's boys had too. So far all efforts to trace Toju had proven abortive. He had taken Mofe up strongly; the boy should have been taken care of before he left the lodge, for there was no saying what the guy would spring up on them. The Lokoja meeting was another emerging problem. The names of those who had attended were being compiled. It wouldn't be long before his name came up too.

His continued stay here didn't seem so wise anymore but Mofe insisted it was the only way to know what the Federal Government knew, Mofe had reasoned with him that the reasons for the Lokoja meeting were still unknown for now, it could be assumed to be harmless. Their only problem was this Toju character. He would keep Mofe informed if Toju was found, it's important we get to him first and kill him, he reasoned. I might also give an order that he be taken dead or alive if he resists arrest by the SSS, that way he'd be killed by either Mofe's boys or the SSS.

The phone on his table rang. He picked it up

"Sir, the President has called for you to see him in the next three hours at the villa", his secretary said.

"Thanks Chinwe, please reschedule my meeting for that time. Also help me get a call through to the Delta State Governor right?"

"Yes sir" she said as he dropped the phone. Chinwe, his secretary had just been transferred from the Supreme Court complex to the presidency. Now that she was so close to the seat of power, David Ajiboye, her lover was not around to hear all the things she'd been seeing. I really do miss him, she thought, he is such a good listener!

CHAPTER NINE

"WALE WHAT DO you think we ought to do about this young man Mofe has decided to eliminate? I'm really not comfortable with it at all! Do you realize we are going to be accessories to murder?" Tekena Tokubiye had gone to see Chief Wale Adekanye in his office.

"See Tekena, you're not the only one oh! I've talked to about two members of our group and they all expressed the same sentiment. I mean commissioning a lawyer to take up a case is one thing but this murder business is another thing entirely, we didn't intend for anyone to lose his life".

"So what are we going to do now? We can't just fold our hands and go to sleep, we must do something. Mofe hasn't called a meeting for sometime now, the last I heard from him, he said Toju had evaded capture by his boys. If he goes silently into exile or something we don't have a problem but I doubt if he would do that. Wale we have to do something and quick too. If Mofe's boys kill him, we're in trouble and if they don't we're still in trouble. We must find a way of untangling ourselves from this mess" said Tokubiye. "So what are you suggesting?" Adekanye asked. "This whole thing was Mofe's idea and Chinedu has been egging him on, I say we find a way of making both of them take the rap for our sakes, why should we all go down? Now that Chinedu is the NSA, it will be very tricky but it's still possible. We must meet the President and tell him what has been going on. We'll just have to give him all the details. We'll tell him we didn't want to be involved in murder and that's why we've come to be straight with him." "I'm sure you know he won't take it easy with us", Adekanye cut in testily,

"We're the ones that orchestrated the events that have most threatened his government, it's because of us his dream of rapid privatization has been stalled, political tension, inflation; you name it we caused it. Do you think he'll just slap us on the wrist and tell us to be good boys? Think man think! We're in this mess as high as our noses! It would be very hard for only Mofe and Chinedu to go down; we'd all go down too".

"I agree but how about if we just fabricate something or the other to frame them, what do you think? Tokubiye asked.

"If we can come up with something that would implicate only both of them I'm in for it. Someone needs to be given up and like you said Chinedu and Mofe fit the bill . . .

** ** ** ** ** ** ** ** **

"You must be joking, right?" Charles Ofili asked Toju after going through the written statement Toju brought to his office. "I'm not joking at all, everything you just read is as factual as the sun rising in the morning," said Toju.

"My God, so this is what these people have been up to. It's so hard to take it all in. How in God's name did you get mixed up with this crowd?

Did you really think you were dealing with patriots?" asked Ofili with an incredulous look on his face.

"Forgive my idealism, I thought they meant well for the people. Now I can clearly see that they had their own agenda. I guess when they realized I actually believed in what I had done they decided to pay me off or at worst kill me or something. One thing that's on my mind now is my feeling there's a connection between my presenting my findings to them and the other crises rocking the nation right now".

"By the way what actually did you find in the 1999 constitution?" Ofili asked. Toju paused and then let out a sigh. He wasn't sure whether to tell him or not, he found it difficult to trust people now.

"For now let's leave that point okay? When I'm sure of what's going on I'll let you know" Ofili was now sufficiently curious, he wanted this story to flow from his desk. I'm just going to have to respect that, he thought, there's no use putting pressure on the poor guy.

"So what do you suggest we do now? Am I to publish what you've given me so far or what?"

"To tell you the truth" Toju said, "I really don't know what to do, as of now you're the only one I've told anything about this except my wife. For now what we have will only be enough to make good copy for Empire newsmagazine, it will expose your flank too you know".

"I guess I'm prepared for that" Ofili said with as much gusto as he could summon, "Have you forgotten the days of guerilla journalism? Without prejudice to the fact that we have democracy, we journalists have still kept all our friendly forces and escape routes intact. There's no telling the day when we have to return to the trenches to expel another dictator. Let's just hope things never get that bad again". "Well let's hope so for all our sakes, I think we should run the story. You can credit it to an unnamed source or something, you guys know how you write such stuff right?" asked Toju. "For sure, I'm on to it immediately. You know what? I'll author the piece personally" Ofili said.

** ** ** ** ** ** ** ** **

Ahmed Jiga was deep in thought in his home in Zaria. The air-conditioning hummed silently, the only sound that could be heard was his ritual of tapping his pen on the table. He had just returned from his second meeting with General Muktar in Abuja. It had gone quite well or so he thought. He hadn't known how to bring any other member of the Northern Elders into the meeting without it being obvious that he was orchestrating the whole thing. All of them are just plain lily-livered, he thought. None of them is ready to even entertain the thought of a coup. He had convinced Muktar of their support nonetheless.

He could see himself being sworn-in as the President of the Federal Republic of Nigeria. It seemed so close he could almost feel it in his bones. Nowadays he seemed so distant to his wives and children. He was always caught in one fantasy or the other, speaking in codes, telling his wives and children to be ready as something big was about to happen that would shoot him to the spotlight. As it is with all megalomaniacs, he increasingly spent time alone dreaming and fantasizing. After working for others all these years his time too had come.

He had concluded plans to inform the Northern Elders about the coup the day before it happened, telling them he had just been briefed about it. He would make them see the need to come together to see how they could protect the interest of "their people". In every bargaining process, he knew, he that has the most information usually gets the best deal. Before they know what had hit them they would see him as the only one to give direction to the northern people. Sometimes he wondered if the northern people ever benefited from the many acts carried out on their behalf to protect the "northern interest" Hum! More like the interests of their leaders. Any way, who cares? The people don't know the difference. Their leaders must give them direction, that's where I come in surely my time has come . . . ." He thought.

** ** ** ** ** ** ** ** **

"How long do you think it will be before I'm found out? Mofe I think I need to resign now" said Chinedu Okafor. He was talking to Mofe Amajuoritse on a secure phone line in his office.

"Just take it easy Chinedu, there's no need to get all worked up. Look, if you've not realized it you're the NSA! You can kill any security report you like. Have you thought about disbanding the team looking into the Lokoja meeting?"

"No I haven't, maybe that's what I'll do. It's easy for you to sound so confident," Okafor charged, "You have your immunity as governor to cover you, I don't have any such immunity".

"I know that's what you are thinking but it's not like that at all" Mofe said. Chinedu was beginning to irritate him.

"Leave that for now. What's the word from your SSS boys, haven't they sighted Toju yet?" "No they haven't," said Okafor "In fact something else has come up, would you believe Ahmed Jiga is actually involved in a coup plot? The bloody opportunist wants to take advantage of the crisis in the country. He tried to involve General Muktar but the man ratted on him. Muktar is convinced Jiga is working alone though he is masquerading like the northerners are behind him" "My God that's serious", Mofe said after some time, "So what are you people planning to do?"

"The President has decided to make sure he is prosecuted, he is determined to prove he is his own man and can take hard decisions against even the most highly placed. I guess Jiga is going to be used to score some political points for the presidents' credibility. He is however not taking any chances. He doesn't want it to seem as if he is against northerners so every effort has been made to get incriminating evidence on Jiga. What we presently have is damning enough", Okafor said

"That is one big star about to fall out of the north's political sky. I hope the President survives the effort", said Mofe.

"I hope so too, they may still not take it lightly with him especially when viewed against the backdrop of the demands Solution 1914 made on them which they have been faithfully implementing, they just might take this Jiga's case as just the last straw. Mofe, somehow I think everything we did has created more problems now than we ever thought".

"Nonsense, don't worry about a thing. Everything will straighten itself out very soon. Try to keep me posted. Call me later in the week. Don't worry we'll come out unscathed". "Alright" Okafor said as he dropped the phone. Instead of being relieved he now seemed even more apprehensive, I do hope I can really come out of this unscathed.

PART FOUR

THE
CURTAINS
FALL

CHAPTER TEN

January 26, 2pm Lagos

David Ajiboye was on his way to Abuja. Things were really looking up. Toju had unknowingly led his men to his hideout in Mushin by withdrawing money from the same branch of his bank on two separate occasions. That was all they had needed to track him down. He had quickly dispatched the news to the NSA's office as he'd been directed to. He then decided to go ahead to prepare the place Toju was to be kept when his men brought him to Abuja. Actually he was only using that as a pretext to see Chinwe. He couldn't explain it himself, he almost felt compelled to see her. Boy you're going soft, he thought to himself.

His men had dropped him off at the domestic wing of the Murtala Muhammad Airport immediately after he had faxed the good news to the NSA. Since his flight was leaving in the next 20 minutes he decided to take a stroll through the shops in the airport while waiting. As he stood looking at the foreign newsstands, his phone rang. He looked at the number, he couldn't place it but he answered the call anyway. "Hello who is this?" asked David.

"This is the National security Adviser, I believe I'm speaking with David Ajiboye am I right". David couldn't believe it,

"Yes you are sir, how may I be of help?" "Yes I wanted to know exactly where you located Toju to be staying". Strange, I thought the big boys didn't like to know the messy details David thought, and then said,

"Cool Me Down Motel on Layi Oyekanmi street Mushin. We are going to pick him up tomorrow morning".

"That's very good. If he resists arrest you shouldn't hesitate to shoot him, do you understand?" asked Okafor. David was wondering what the hell was going on, when did politicians begin to tell us how to do our job? He calmly replied

"We know what to do sir, don't worry",

"That's very good; I just wanted to be sure, take care then. Goodbye and keep up the good work", Okafor said before he dropped the phone.

David was beginning to feel just a bit uneasy, why should the NSA call to know exactly where Toju was? Why the order not to hesitate to shoot? He wanted to call his men and tell them not to hesitate to shoot but he stopped himself, that's so silly. Rather he'd call them and tell them to try by all means to bring in the man alive. They probably shouldn't even wait till tomorrow; they should bring him in today. Damn these politicians!

Imagine the gall, trying to teach me how to do my job! If it were not that he'd told Chinwe he was coming, he would stay in Lagos to bring Toju in personally. He still felt uneasy; something had unsettled him during that call from the NSA. Something's not right about this, he just couldn't figure out what.

** ** ** ** ** ** ** ** **

6:57 pm, Lagos.

What a boring day, Toju was thinking. He had stayed indoors all day, finally getting used to the sound of cockroaches crawling on the carpet in his motel room in Mushin. He'd talked with Jumoke earlier in the day and briefed her about his meeting with Ofili. The story would hit the newsstands in two days. Every thing was set. The only thing was that he couldn't move around as freely as he would have liked. He had read and reread all the newspapers he'd sent one of the bar boys to buy for him. Maybe I should just take a stroll, at least I'm safe here, he thought.

Unknown to him, two men were seated in a white Peugeot 504 parked a few meters away from Cool Me Down Motel, waiting for nightfall before they would go into the motel and shoot Toju. One of them had seen Toju on the day he had gone to the governor's lodge after returning from Abuja.

He had led Toju to the boardroom for that briefing with Solution 1914. The other man was a personal bodyguard to Mofe Amajuoritse and also an expert driver. They had been given their marching orders to silence Toju forever. It hadn't been hard locating the motel; the driver knew Lagos streets like the back of his hand.

Layi Oyekanmi Street is one of the longest streets in Mushin; it connects the Ilasamaja end of Mushin to another road that connects commuters moving from Mushin to Isolo. David Ajiboye's" men had parked their car on one of the side streets linked to Layi Oyekanmi. They had left the car and blended into the environment as much as possible. They had their eyes on the motel; once it became a little dark they would go in and get Toju. David had called to tell them to ensure they bring Toju in alive. They'd spent quality time mastering Toju's pictures; they could pick him out of a semi-lit room. The stage was set for the ensuing drama.

Toju came down the stairs telling Wale the bartender he was going for a stroll. He stopped by the gate to buy some sweets from the Mallams' kiosk that was just outside the gate. There was a fluorescent tube located just by the kiosk; it provided just enough illumination for the men in the white 504 to see that their man was going out. The SSS agents saw him too and signaled to each other.

Suddenly the short man seated by the driver of the 504 got out and started walking towards the motel, he had to cross the road to get to Toju. He reached into his trouser pocket to pull out a. 45-caliber pistol that he held closely to his side as he crossed the street. One of the SSS agents had also started walking towards Toju. He was nearly there when he noticed the gun in the hand of the man crossing the street. In that split second Toju looked up and found he was staring into a familiar face. As it dawned on him from where he knew the man, the SSS agent shouted, "Toju get down!" as he pulled out his own gun. The first shot rang out just as Toju turned round to get back into the motel. The mallam at the kiosk took to his heels, as did everyone in the immediate vicinity. The short man ran after Toju, the SSS agent was in hot pursuit.

Toju's mind was racing almost as wildly as his feet, they'd found him and were going to kill him, dear God I'm too young to die!. If he could just get to his room and bolt the door probably he could get some minutes to get out through the window. This thought energized him as he took the stairs three at a time. As he got to the landing, he pulled out his keys and started fumbling for his room key. Suddenly the short man was on the landing too, he pointed his gun straight at Toju. He froze. There was a volley of two gunshots. The short man crumpled to the floor, his blood oozing out of the holes at the back of his head. The SSS agent had shot him. Toju just sat on the floor dazed, looking at the dead man lying prostrate a few meters from where he was.

The SSS agent stepped over the body and walked over to Toju, still clutching his smoking pistol.

"Mr. Omatsone, you will have to follow us. My name is Peter Oshadu; I'm with the SSS". Toju merely nodded his head. His close brush with death had knocked the fight out of him.

The second agent climbed the stairs, Oshadu turned to him and asked, "Where's the other man?" "As soon as he saw me coming he started the car and zoomed off," he said. Oshadu nodded his head and said,

"Let's pick his personal effects from the room and get out of here".

      **   **   **   **   **   **   **   **   **

9pm, Abuja

David had been with Chinwe since he got to Abuja. He had gone to her place after making the arrangements for the chalet they would keep Toju in Maitama district. He had missed Chinwe's warm embraces. They had spent quality time reestablishing that particular aspect of their love affair. Chinwe got up from the bed and announced,

"I want to go cook something for us". David mumbled something she couldn't hear. After tossing around for some minutes he got up and followed her to the kitchen.

"You said something about being transferred, where are you now?" he asked as he sat on a stool in the kitchen. Chinwe immediately warmed to the topic, "Yes . . . I'm at the Presidency now. Aso Rock itself! It's so much fun seeing the high and mighty at such close range. I'm the secretary to Chinedu Okafor the National security Adviser." Toju was a bit stunned, if Chinwe had been looking at him she'd have seen the look on his face, fortunately she was busy peeling some yams.

"He's such a nice man" she continued

"Whenever I need the day off he rarely objects. One thing I can't understand about him is the way he's always making phone calls. I've never known a man that makes as much calls as he does. I thought we women were the ones always on the phone!"

"Always making calls you say? He must be quite a family man" said Ajiboye cautiously. He was trying to probe her for details. "Family man? Please! I think he's only called his wife a few times since I got here. He seems to be quite close to the Delta state governor. Its either the NSA's calling him or he is calling the NSA. Sometimes they talk as much as two or three times a day. You know these politicians; they're always up to something"

By now David was perplexed, the Delta State Governor? He just couldn't believe it. A man we are investigating for likely treasonable offenses against the state is the bosom pal of the NSA? What kind of government is this? Chinwe broke into his thoughts,

"David what's the matter you look worried?" She had stopped peeling the yams and walked over to where he sat.

"I'm okay" he said as she put her arm around him. He stood and said,

"I'm feeling a bit tired maybe I should just lie down". He walked out of the kitchen and headed for the bedroom. He closed the door behind him and got out his cell phone. His boys ought to be in Abuja by now he thought.

He dialed Oshadu's number; it rang twice and was picked.

"Peter, is the man with you?" Ajiboye asked.

"Yes sir, he's with us. We were actually just on time; apparently some other people were there for him too. They were there to kill him sir". David sighed deeply; it all made sense now, our position is being compromised, he thought.

"Peter I want you to take Toju some place else, don't take him to the place in Maitama. Any safe place will do and make sure you don't contact anyone, reply no calls except for mine. When you are settled, call me and tell me where you are, understand?"

"Yes sir I do" Peter said and then asked

"Is there something wrong sir, why all the precautions?" "Just do what I said, when we see I'll fill you in. Now get to it". David cut the call and picked up his small travel bag, Chinwe's going to be disappointed tonight he thought.

**   **   **   **   **   **   **   **   **

11:27pm, Abuja

"What do you mean he wasn't taken?" screamed Chinedu Okafor,

"How could he escape again?". He was with Mofe Amajuoritse who was in Abuja for a Council of State meeting. Amajuoritse calmly took a sip from his glass of orange juice, dropped it, looked at Okafor and said

"Exactly what does it sound like I mean? I said he wasn't taken. Apparently your SSS boys were there too and bungled the whole thing. Only the driver got away, the other man is dead". He picked his juice again and continued sipping from it.

"How can you be so relaxed? Can't you see the games up? They've gotten him, it won't be long before he spills the beans. Oh my God, we're done for!" Okafor slumped in his chair from sheer physical and mental exhaustion. He could hardly sleep nowadays; he was always worrying about what would be the outcome of this whole crazy experience.

He silently cursed the day he'd gotten involved with Solution 1914. Can you just imagine, thought Okafor as he looked at Amajuoritse who was sitting across from him, the man doesn't seem worried in the slightest way.

"So what are we going to do now" he finally asked.

"I was waiting for you to get to that part" Amajuoritse said

"For now there is nothing we can do. Have you heard from your boys? They ought to report where they're taking him to right"

"Yes I'm sure at least by tomorrow morning they ought to fax me the latest news," said Okafor somberly.

"I don't think Toju will tell them anything, he will be too scared, not knowing if he can trust them. The only thing would be if they get suspicious about how our boys knew where to get Toju. For now we must wait and watch till we hear from them. When I get back from the Council meeting tomorrow I expect to hear from you. Till then I think you ought to get some sleep, you look like a wreck. Relax man. We'll sort things out".

Okafor tried to take some comfort in those words but he couldn't. He got up as gracefully as he could and said,

"You're right everything will sort itself out. We'll see tomorrow then. "They shook hands and Okafor was on his way home, thinking of how he could extricate himself from the whole thing.

Chapter Eleven

January 27, Aso Rock Abuja, 11:15am

THE COUNCIL OF STATE meeting had been on for about 2 hours already. Several thorny issues had been thrashed and the meeting already seemed to be coming to a predicable end. The President cleared his throat to subtly call attention back to himself,

"There is one more issue I would like to bring to the attention of the Council of State". All discussion ceased and all eyes were on the President, the seriousness in the tone of his voice gave the indication that what was coming was not too pleasant.

"It is said that for every twelve there is a Judas. It is almost impossible for me to understand the motivations of some of the citizens of this country. The naked desire for power and glory seems to have deprived otherwise good men of their senses". By this time everyone in the room was on the edge of their seat in anticipation.

"Gentlemen, I have in my possession incontrovertible proof that a coup was in the offing to oust the present civilian administration".

"A coup?" The immediacy of that thought didn't go too well with some of those present, especially those of purely civilian backgrounds.

"These elements have sought to take advantage of the unfortunate circumstances and challenges faced by this administration in the recent past" said the President.

"Who are those involved in this plot? "asked the Senate President.

"The search for other likely co-conspirators is still on but for now we have only one definite suspect. He is none other than the immediate past National security Adviser, Alhaji Jiga".

"Unbelievable!" said one of the northern governors; others around the room were voicing similar and dissenting sentiments. The side comments continued until the President cleared his throat again.

"As we speak, an order has been given for his arrest and eventual prosecution for treasonable felony. Let me make it clear that this administration will not fail or falter in its responsibility of protecting the sanctity of our hard won democracy. We will not hesitate to deal with anyone" at this point the President looked in the direction of Mofe Amajuoritse, who coolly gazed back, "who is found to be working at cross purposes to the wishes and desires of the elected government of Nigeria. There shall be no sacred cows".

From then on the President proceeded to outline to the Council of State what kind of evidence they had against Jiga. He explained to them that he had wanted them to hear about it before a statement to the press was made. The meeting ended with a prayer and those present began doing what politicians do best. The President called Chinedu Okafor over to see him. As they shook hands, the President asked,

"Chinedu, come I've not heard from you for sometime now? Are you okay? You look tired" Okafor tried to summon a winning smile,

"I'm okay sir, just too many late nights taking their toll on me." The President asked his aide who was standing nearby,

"What's next on my schedule?" "You have a meeting with Chief Adekanye in three hours time".

"Put Chinedu next in line to see me after that" said the President to his aide then he said,

"Chinedu see me by 2:30 okay. I'll see you later then" Chinedu was left wondering what exactly the President knew. He had probably been the only other person to notice the President's look in the direction of the Delta State Governor.

** ** ** ** ** ** ** ** **

Wuse, Abuja. 11:25am

"Now that we know the role the NSA is playing, how should we proceed?" asked Peter Oshadu. They had brought Toju to a house belonging to an old friend of Oshadu. They now sat in conference reviewing the situation together. David Ajiboye, Oshadu, Toju and Uche Obi, the third man in Ajiboye's team were sipping their chilled drinks on the dining table. They had spent time piecing together all what Toju and David knew about the events leading up to the attempt on Toju's life. Toju was especially amazed at how unsuspecting he had been throughout the period David had been on his trail.

"It's obvious going through the NSA's office is out of it" said Toju, "We must let the President know directly. He ought to be briefed directly. There's no saying what other mischief that Okafor fellow is up to in the

Presidency. He must be stopped at once". David nodded his head in agreement and said,

"He must be stopped but how? Don't you know how impossible it is for a small fry like me in the SSS to get to see the President?"

"How about the DG of the SSS?" asked Toju. "He's on leave and his assistant is womanizing in Port-Harcourt as we speak" Uche Obi answered.

"Blast it" said Toju as he hit his fist on the table "The rot in this country is unbelievable"

"There is something we could do" said David as he leaned forward in his chair, all the others leaned forward, all eager to grasp some hope.

"I have a friend from way back in my activist days who is now one of the President's aides. He gave me his card recently, I hope I'm still with it" David said as he brought out his wallet from his trouser pocket and rummaged through it. He found it,

"This is it, let me go and try his mobile phone number, we've got nothing to lose" he said as he got up and walked to the sitting room where the phone was.

He came back after a few minutes all smiles,

"We're in! He's arranged for two people to see the President in two hours time, I guess that's Toju and I. If I believed in God, at this point I'd say hallelujah!". You're already on your way to faith", Toju said grinning from ear to ear,

"Mark my words"

** ** ** ** ** ** ** ** **

Maitama, Abuja 11:28am

"He asked me to see him at 2:30pm. Do you think he knows something we don't?" Chinedu Okafor asked Mofe Amajuoritse who was pacing the sitting room of the governor's lodge like a trapped tiger.

"How the hell should I know? You're the NSA, I should be asking you!" shouted Mofe, his cool demeanor had been ship wrecked by the presidents' thinly veiled threat during the Council of State meeting.

Okafor was secretly pleased, at last he's getting the feel of the situation, he thought to himself: Mofe broke into his thoughts

"So have they reported yet? We need to know where they're keeping him so we can make sure to kill him now. There's no chance for slip-ups now."

"They haven't sent in a report yet, I checked my office immediately after the council meeting I tried calling the team leader but it keeps telling me his phone is switched off, I don't know what to do next", said Okafor wringing his hands, the very picture of anxiety. "Have you heard from any of our members, Solution 1914 I mean" asked Okafor. "No I haven't" Mofe snapped back,

"They have not returned my calls either. Their behavior is beginning to bother me"

"There was something I wanted to tell you but I can't remember what, I know it has got to do with Solution 1914. Ha am I getting old?" said Okafor as he scratched his baldhead.

"Well just make sure you remember soon enough", Mofe said as he glanced at his watch,

"I have a meeting with the Warri Ladies Vanguard Abuja branch now and it should last for about two hours or so. I guess we won't see again till after your meeting with the President. Till then, stay alive and alert, if your SSS boys contact you, make sure to call me immediately so I can send my boys to take care of things. See you later". He walked out of the room leaving Okafor staring at his retreating form. Okafor felt like he was left to do the dirty dishes. When I'm out of this mess I'll make sure I deal with this fellow, he thought,

** ** ** ** ** ** ** ** **

Aso Rock, Abuja, 1.00pm

Toju and David had been duly cleared at the gates. Just seeing his name on the Presidents "expected" list put a little more bounce in David's' step as they walked the corridors of power. Toju was indifferent to it all, the whole ambience of power was rubbing him the wrong way. Just look at all these unnecessary furnishings, just another contract for these fat cats to execute. He had finally come to the conclusion that all politicians were the same, east, west, north and south, they were all rogues. They would come together to feast on the nations' resources then they'd turn the people against each other using religious or ethnic sentiment when they had been outsmarted by their fellows. For now his own survival was high on his mind.

They were ushered into a well furnished room and told to wait for his Excellency. David noticed another door on the other side of the room, I guess that's where he's going to come in through, he thought. They both sat in silence, lost in their individual thoughts. The side door opened and in walked the President accompanied by the Vice President and David's friend, the presidential aide. He's even taller than I thought, Toju said to himself. They shook hands and sat down.

"So what is this all about? What's so important that you have to see me personally?" asked the President. Toju motioned for David to speak. He proceeded to explain the scenario as it stood. The President and Vice President broke in from to time to time to ask clarifying questions but were largely quiet throughout the time David was speaking.

By the time David finished the President had broken into a sweat and his skin had gone clammy despite the air conditioning. He looked at the V.P and said,

"This is the last straw, can you believe it? Chinedu of all people! First Jiga, now Chinedu, where will it all end?" "Did you mention Chief Wale Adekanye as one of the members of that 1914 group?" asked the V.P.

"Yes, he's a member of solution 1914" answered Toju.

"I'm supposed to be meeting him in the next thirty minutes or so" said the President with a bewildered look on his face.

"I know that's why I asked", said the V.P.

"What did he say his mission was?". "A private matter he said but an important one nevertheless. I'm also supposed to see Chinedu after Adekanye, I guess, the chickens are all coming home to roost. We'll let them say their piece and hang themselves. Get me the Justice Minister, I need to know what offenses these people can be convicted of; none of them should go scot-free. That includes you young man", the President said pointing at Toju,

"what did you think you were doing accepting a brief like that? You are one of the people troubling Nigeria!" Toju flared up in an instant, all the resentment he'd had bottled up came to the surface

"No you and your kind are the "troublers" of Nigeria! Maybe my choice of the people to work with was wrong but certainly my objective remains noble. You people have sat on the wealth of our people and grown fat on it. If you would just stop there it won't be so bad but you proceed to turn brothers against themselves all in the name of marginalization both ethnic and religious! You then stay far away from the scene of the battle. May God deal with you people! The blood of untold number of innocent citizens is crying out against you and your kind! I tell you without a doubt you will still pay for it. If you can get an offense to pin on me, I'd face it with all dignity but I assure you, you won't"

David couldn't believe the rage coming from Toju. Everyone was silent, even the President, known for his own sharp tongue, was strangely silent. A man who actually believes something was a wonder to behold, a rarity in Abuja where alignments of expedience and convenience were the rule rather than the exception.

"We will look into your case in due course", said the President in a much subdued voice,"

"For now we must hear from Adekanye, I have a feeling what he has say to say is relevant to the issues at hand".

** ** ** ** ** ** ** ** **

Aso Rock, Abuja, 1:38pm

"So you see sir, I decided to alert you on these things so that you will know the forces working against your administration. As a patriotic Nigerian, I could not just stand back and see these enemies of progress ruin your sincere efforts to move the nation forward." Adekanye took in some air; he had been talking nonstop for about ten minutes.

The V.P. was looking at him in a strange way; he couldn't decipher what the look meant. The President himself looked slightly bored. "Is that all?" the President finally asked. "Yes sir". "How did you discover this conspiracy between Chinedu Okafor and Mofe Amajuoritse?" Adekanye leaned forward in a most conspiratorial manner and said,

"My sources are confidential but reliable, for now I can't reveal them; I just came to let you know about it. They are up to no good, the sooner we deal with them the better". The President leaned forward too, he said

"What if I tell you I already know everything you just told me and much more?" Adekanye broke into a sweat, he didn't know what to make of that, the President didn't even give him a chance to respond before saying,

"You're a foolish man chief, do you know that? I know all about you and Solution 1914" At this time Adekanye knew he was in trouble.

"Sir I can explain everything." The V.P. raised his hand signaling him to silence.

"Wale I can't believe you're so stupid. So you mean you knew all this and were still smiling to my face? With friends like you I don't need enemies". He picked up the receiver of the intercom and said,

"Let them in" Adekanye just sat staring at the Executive duo

"I can explain everything "he said

Toju and David walked in. Toju and Adekanye's eyes looked on each other, Toju glared at him. Adekanye broke eye contact, I know this man, he thought to himself.

"I can see there's no need for introductions, the V.P. said,

"Now Chief Adekanye, you will do yourself a big favor by coming clean with us right now. There's only one thing we need to know from you right now. This young man presented your group with his findings, after that he didn't hear from you till you tried to make him forget the case. He believes you have some how used that report nonetheless. Now I want you to give us the details of what you did with it and you had better tell the whole truth" Chief Adekanye thought for a moment, he had no choice. He sang.

** ** ** ** ** ** ** ** **

Aso Rock, Abuja 2:26pm

Chinedu Okafor was on his way out of his office as one of the presidential aides walked through the door of Chinwe's office.

"The President is ready to see you sir, you can come with me" said the aide. He turned to Chinwe and said,

"I'll be going home from there, if I get any calls direct them to my mobile number. I'll see you tomorrow then".

"Have a good day sir", Chinwe said cheerily as the NSA walked out.

He was led into a large sitting room the President used when receiving very large foreign delegations. To his left sat the President and Vice President on one settee, Toju, David and Prof. Isaac Dogo the Attorney general and justice minister were sitting to his right. Chief Wale Adekanye sat on a separate settee directly facing Okafor. He was led to this settee by the aide who eventually left the room. "Welcome Chinedu" was the presidents' curt greeting,

"We've been waiting for you". Okafor surveyed the room. He didn't even acknowledge Adekanye, who was seating beside him, his eyes rested on Toju. For a brief second he felt like making a quick move for the door. There's no use, he thought, I should have known it would come to this. He sat in silence, head bowed as he fiddled with the breast pocket of his safari suit.

"To say I'm disappointed in you would be an understatement. I brought you into my government to rehabilitate you politically and just see how you have repaid me? Chinedu, I fear men like you. I understand our tendency as politicians to plan and scheme for our advantage but yours is an especially despicable kind. For a few deals to line your pockets you were willing to play with the lives of millions of Nigerians? Chief Adekanye has given us the gory details so I won't bother to ask you anything. Or do you think you have something to say in your own defense?" asked the President. All eyes fell on the NSA, he looked from one face to the other, in reality he felt no shame for his actions. He was only regretting the fact that he allowed himself to be caught. He finally spoke,

"What can I say? There it is. Everything I did, I did out of necessity. There's no point trying to sound saintly about the whole thing".

"Everything out of necessity eh?" asked Toju,

"Getting me killed was also part of necessity right?"

"I will not respond to that," Okafor said, he'd figured out the need to stay silent on that particular point.

"You don't have to respond to it", Prof. Dogo cut in.

"You will be placed under arrest for the attempted murder of Mr. Toritseju Omatsone. I'm sure you can afford a good lawyer, you'll need one"

Chapter Twelve

CRY, THE BETRAYED COUNTRY
BY CHARLES OFILI

THREE WEEKS AGO, the Empire newsmagazine broke the exclusive story of the subterranean moves of the organization called Solution 1914. Reactions to that editions' cover story were immediate. Our phones were ringing nonstop, letters and emails came in by the minute, text messages assaulted the tranquility of the private homes of our staff. From rounded condemnation to heightened applause, reactions were impassioned and unrelenting.

I have personally learnt something from the events that accompanied that edition. It was basically my discovery of the fickleness of our political class. Some of those we named as members of Solution 1914 first denied their membership and then backpedaled when it seemed some Nigerians supported what they stood for. Reliable sources have given the explanation for the most recent volte-face, denying membership: *Likely prosecution for economic sabotage of the privatization process.*

Early this week, Engineer Chinedu Okafor, the erstwhile National Security Adviser and member of Solution 1914 was charged to court alongside Mofe Amajuoritse, Governor of Delta State for the attempted murder of one Toritseju Omatsone. Mr. Omatsone is the mystery "whistle blower" in this weird tale unfolding before the stunned Nigerian populace. The majority of ordinary citizens are hailing his act of courage in exposing the corrupt underbelly of Nigerian politics. The immunity enjoyed by serving state governors as provided for by the 1999 constitution seems to be the cog in the wheel of the successful prosecution of Mofe Amajuoritse. Even this may soon cease to be a hindrance to the course of justice as the political class, at least in Delta State, seems set to redeem itself. The State House of Assembly has begun impeachment proceedings against the Governor for gross misconduct. This is to clear the way for his prosecution.

As if the good citizens of Nigeria had not had enough disgusting news about the political class already, we were stunned to receive the news of the arrest and arraignment of Chinedu Okafor's predecessor as NSA, Alhaji Aminu Jiga for treasonable felony. Our reporter, Sade Ogidan, spoke to him last week as he got out of the dock in an Abuja High Court. His usually ebullient self was gone, he spotted an unshaved beard, and he'd lost weight and a great part of his aristocratic swagger. When quizzed on his chances of regaining his freedom he said,

"Without a doubt my chances are very bright. You can't keep a good man down. It is obvious to all concerned that I'm innocent of all charges. Whoever heard of only one man being tried for coup plotting? Where are my fellow coup plotters? It's all a big conspiracy against my person, they re not happy with my rising profile". The Attorney–general, Prof. Isaac Dogo is leading the prosecution team personally. When asked to comment he said,

"We have a cast iron case against him. It should actually be a walkover". So there it is and the man on the street in left wondering who is telling the truth. A strange twist in the tale emerged as a meeting of Northern elders rose to roundly condemn Jiga's role in the botched coup attempt. Their spokesman, Alhaji Ahmed Muazu said in Kaduna, "I am not surprised at these charges leveled against him. We've known all along that he was an opportunist. He ought to face the music squarely". When asked if he thought Jiga's arraignment was the first move in a plan to attack northerners, he replied, "Not in the least, I don't think so, Jiga is an embarrassment to us, he doesn't represent any of our interests. Informed sources say there has been no love lost between Jiga and Muazu before now.

The President has quite surprisingly tried to keep the press informed on issues as they unfold. Some close aides say he has been really shaken by the sordid events now being revealed about his two former NSA's. A cabinet reshuffle is being rumored. The word is out that the President is seriously shopping for credible people to work for him now. While in New York for a UN meeting he had been asked about his personal reaction to the scandals rocking the nation, he said,

"Really I feel betrayed as a person and of course as the President. The Nigerian people all feel betrayed by their leaders. It would take some structural changes to restore this confidence in our people but I can assure you I'm willing to make the necessary changes".

And so there we have it from the lips of the Number one citizen himself. We feel betrayed and used by those we look up to for leadership. **Cry, the betrayed country**. Her citizens are nothing but pawns in the big political chess games our leaders play. They are expendable cartridges in the submachine gun that is the greed of our leaders. But one good thing that has emerged from the events of the last few weeks is the greater awareness that issues like the Sharia controversy and resource control agitation are largely used by politicians to their own benefit – Mr. Omatsone has taken it upon himself to begin the sensitization campaign to reach the masses with this message: Refuse being used by politicians to further their own ends. He is being joined by pro-democracy groups and citizen rights NGO's I interviewed him a few days ago and he had this to say,

"It will not be an easy task but it is one I hope to dedicate the rest of my life to. Our people must understand that the suffering of the man on the street knows no ethnic group or religious belief, poverty is present with all. What the Ijaw fisherman who has been dispossessed of his fishing waters by oil spillage suffers is not too different from the Hausa man who is denied upward mobility by the neatly packaged lies by his "area big man" also suffers. The same frustration mounts in the hearts of both men. It is this frustration that opportunistic politicians take advantage of to set erstwhile neighbors against themselves. My brother, it is so sad. I myself was once rabidly anti-north until I came to realize that the oppressors are never really concerned with such differences. East, West, North or south, they are all the same.

The feeling is Orwellian. On the last page of his book, those poor animals in George Orwell's Animal Farm spied through the window only to see that their rulers, the pigs and the humans, who the pigs had taught them to hate, were now playing a game of cards. To their utmost amazement, the pigs began to look like the humans and vice versa.

I believe we can expose them for what they really are, and then our people can begin to make informed choices about their own well-being. It is a war against ignorance, a war by means and for ends that may at first seem impossible but we will eventually overcome"

Sounds like a man on a mission. With more men like this, I believe the nation may actually stand a chance. But will he be allowed to succeed? Time will tell. All may not be lost for the betrayed country. May she one day arise from the ashes like the proverbial phoenix. The eagle will fly again!